AF654236

The Baby Quail Who Could Not Fly Away

Om KIDZ
An imprint of Om Books International

Once upon a time, there lived a baby quail. He had small feet and wings but could not walk or fly just yet. His parents brought back food for him to their nest and fed him lovingly from their beaks.

Forest fires were common where these birds nested. One day, there was a forest fire. At the first signs of smoke, all the birds began flying away from their nests.

“Save yourselves while you can,” the other birds urged the parents of the baby quail as they left their nests. But the baby quail’s parents refused to

abandon him even as the fire approached the tree in which they had their nest. But as the fire reached the nest, they were forced to flee to save their lives.

The little baby quail, left alone in the nest, watched all the trees catch fire and burn. He also observed that the forest fire had destroyed everything that lay in its path and was out of control now.

"I can do nothing to save myself now as I can't fly away like the other birds," the baby quail thought helplessly. Then he thought about his parents.

“My parents loved me so much. They built a nest for me and always fed me before they ate themselves. They stayed with me till the very last moment and did not fly away earlier like the other birds.

They only flew away when they realised that I could not be saved and they would die too if they stayed back," thought the baby quail.

“I thank my parents for all their love and I pray that they are safe now and happy in the future. I also hope that all the other birds and creatures that have been trapped by the forest fire are safe and unharmed!”

The baby quail prayed for everyone's safety. "I am all alone here, now, and although I have feet, I cannot run away. Even though I have wings, I'm not capable of flying to safety. But I can still think.

"I have a mind that is pure and that functions unlike my wings and my feet. My mind tells me that I haven't harmed anyone. So, I have nothing to fear. It also tells me that I have an innocent truthfulness within me."

Then, a great miracle took place.

God noticed the innocent truthfulness of the baby quail and was moved. God made sure that the new-born truthfulness of the baby quail was merged with the ancient purity of wholesomeness and the Power of Truth.

"May the baby quail who could not fly away and all the birds and other beings that are trapped by the forest fire be saved immediately!" God declared. "Let this forest be safe from such forest fires for a period of a million years!"

And so it came to be!